Elysian Tales

an anthology on Feminism

Elysian Tales:
an anthology on Feminism

Compiled by *Mosiur Rehman*

Edited by *Syeda Faiza Rasheed*

Woven Words Publishers OPC Pvt. Ltd.
Registered Office:
Vill: Raipur, P.O: Raipur Paschimbar,
Dist: Purba Midnapore, Pin: 721401,
West Bengal, India.
www.wovenwordspublishers.net
Email: editor@wovenwordspublishers.net

First published by Woven Words Publishers OPC Pvt. Ltd., 2017

Copyright© Reserved, 2017

ISBN-13: 978-93-86897-03-9
ISBN-10: 9386897032

ANTHOZINE

Price: ₹200

Printed and bound in India

Dedicated to the 70th year of Indian Independence

Contents

1. Sketch — *Aarohy Kapoor*
2. Ink on Lives — *Rida Mohammadi*
3. I want to be ME — *Rida Mohammadi*
4. Shakti — *Sneha Pandey*
5. Testament of Courage — *Arshita Singh*
6. Woman — *Sneha Pandey*
7. Feminism — *Sneha Pandey*
8. Empowered — *Dr. Roopleen*
9. Weak? Warrior? Woman!! — *Sonal Jain*
10. Only if — *Sana Sheikh*
11. The changing face of feminism — *Richika Rastogi*
12. The woman she knew, the story she did not — *Arpita Gupta*
13. Expulsion — *Ayush Ashish*
14. Afterglow — *Fatma Naqvi*
15. You go, girl!! — *Nandini Saxena*
16. My verdict — *kruthika Reddy*
17. Woman-raped??? — *Samrudhi Dash*
18. Yes! She is a woman — *Simran Sharma*
19. Liberated — *Bhooma Bhagat*
20. Woman: The Diamond Dust — *Bandana Kar*
21. The girl next door — *Aarohy Kapoor*
22. For I am a woman? — *Shabbirhusein K*
23. Feminism — *Suman Gupta*
24. I am an ocean — *Deepali Gupta*
25. The voice of an ironman — *Ummesalma*
26. Deepa's dream — *Sonali Basu*
27. Queens in armour — *Ashi Kalim*
28. I am sorry to be born — *Ashi Kalim*
29. I am born again — *Ashi Kalim*
30. 64 cups of elixir — *Kabir Deb*
31. She is — *Pallavi Singh*
32. I cry — *Vinod Gairola*
33. Yes, I am a feminist — *Tanvi Taparia*
34. I, woman — *Sonal Jain*
35. एक अँधेरी रात — *Riya Jain*
36. ना आने की खुशी थी ना जाने का ग़म था.. — *Riya Jain*
37. The Girl cries — *Swastik Anand*
38. Ananya — *Prerna Asthana*
39. A Letter to Girls — *Preiksha Jain*
40. Dear Zindegi, A wish — *Josh*

- *By Aarohy Kapoor*

Ink on Lives

"Madam, you have a patient in E.R. She had a 3 inches lacerated wound on the left side of her forehead, I have stitched it and given inj. T.T 0.5cc IM."said my intern,

"Good job Dr. Pooja, did you ask for the history?"

"No ma'am, the attenders did not let me ask anything to the patient. I need your help."

"It's okay. I will handle it from here, good job!"

I didn't wait for her reply, I made my way towards E.R. A girl of around 15, was lying on the bed. Surrounded by her family. She was crying hard, anyone would think she is crying because of pain, but I knew better. I realised there is something else going on here. You would not feel pain, when you have been stitched under local anaesthesia. I have to get her alone and talk to her privately.

"Alright, I request the guardians to go out. I have to examine the patient."

They moved out very reluctantly.

"Hello Rubina. My name is Dr. Khatija, and I would like to know how did you sustain this injury?"

"Doctor I was playing with my twin brother, we had a brawl. When he pushed me, I fell down and stumbled on the rock."

I would have believed her, but the defeated look in her eyes screamed a different story.

"Rubina, I know you are lying. Now please tell me the truth."

"I got distinction in my 10th exams. I worked so hard. I got accepted in one of the most reputed colleges in the city, but my parents refused for my higher education. My brother barely passed, and they are paying lakhs of donation for his college studies. This is so unfair. I want to study and achieve something. When I demanded this, things got out of hand and my mom slapped me. She didn't mean to hit me so hard, I know that. I just lost balance and hit my head on the kitchen cupboard."

At that time, I just prescribed the medication and sent her home. The whole day I couldn't concentrate on work. When evening rolled, I noted down her address and went to her home directly.

They were surprised to find me there. Even worried. Rubina's mother welcomed me and asked me sit in the living room. The house was smaller than any average house. Three families lived in the house. One by one all came to greet me.

Soon all the children were asked to leave. Rubina's parents, grandfather, two uncles and their wives remained.

"Doctor we aren't trying to be rude, but what is the reason behind this visit?"

It was the grandfather who inquired.

"Mr. Sheikh, I know how Rubina sustained the injury?"

"Oh, so what are you going to do with the information?"

"No, I am not going to do anything. I just want to ask you to reconsider your decision about her studies."

"Last I checked, it's none of your business doctor. Please leave," said her uncle. I wanted to slap him hard and put some sense into his thick head. But that isn't the way to deal with these sort of problems. I needed to be calm and collected.

"She is brilliant and good at studies. Please give her a chance and let her continue."

"Young lady, in our house we don't encourage further education."

"But Rahil has got the permission to study further."

"That's because Rahil is a boy and Rubina is a girl."

This time it was one of the aunt who voiced her opinion.

"So what? Girl or boy, both deserve to get good education."

"Being a Muslim how can you say such an absurd thing? You, members of the younger generation have no respect for the religion. Always doing things against Islam and rebelling. Allah will never forgive you. You will be among the hell-dwellers. In the name of modernization and development you girls stray away from the righteous path. And I pity your parents, they must be ashamed of having a daughter like you. Don't brainwash our daughter's mind and butt into our business."

That did it. He crossed the limits, uncle or not, he is so going to get it.

"Excuse me Mr. Athaulla Sheikh, you don't begin to preach Islam to me. What do you know about Islam? Islam never oppressed the girls.

Talabul-ilmi-faridhatun-muslimeen-wa-muslimaatun.

That means, seeking knowledge is an obligation upon every Muslim - men and women.

It isn't me who is a shame to our religion. It is people like you, who know nothing about Islam and spoil the name of our religion. It is just an excuse people like you have created to oppress girls and keep women from their basic rights like education, choice of marriage, work and earning.

Stop being a hypocrite and treat your daughters and sons equally. And education is the fundamental right of women.

Mrs. Nauhera Sheikh, you are the mother, do you want your child to have a life like you? Always depending on others. Never having a life of her own?

Mr. Adnan Sheikh, think about it. And provide a better life to your daughter. Don't listen to others, take the right decision.

Grandfather, aren't you the one who demanded at the reception for a lady doctor to treat your granddaughter? If everyone stops their daughters from education, then we won't have any lady doctors.

And for your information, my parents are proud of me."

They all looked ashamed. Later they confessed another reason, they didn't want to waste so much money on a girl. For that I advised them about the scholarships and bid goodbye.

With a hope I left their house, and decided to provide the same hope to as many as possible.

8years later,

"Doctor, we have a patient in E.R. A girl had consumed 20 paracetamol tablets, as her parents refused to send her to the college. I have given stomach wash and started I.V. line."

"Good job Dr. Rubina Sheikh."

- ***By Rida Mohammadi***, *Mysore based doctor and*
writer

I want to be ME

I don't need a hero to rescue me,

For I am not a damsel in distress.

I don't need a man to pay my bills,

For I am not a charity case.

I don't want to be an equal to any man,

For I just want to find my own place.

I don't want to compete with you,

For I just want to win my own battles.

I don't care what you think of me,

For I live my life with my own rules.

I don't want you to judge me,

For I am busy fighting my own demons.

I don't want you to dictate my life,

For I know what I want and I am going to get it.

Yes, I am a feminist,

I deserve what you deserve,

But I am not going to beg you for it.

I don't want to be measured in your standards,

I just want to be left alone and I want to be ME.

By Rida Mohammadi

Shakti

Every voice,

Every thought,

Every conscience,

Every breath,

Is hers.

The life in every cell of living,

The manifestation of existence forming.

The gentle and the loving,

The fierce but forgiving.

Is all her.

You see her every day.

The fire in her eyes,

The determined will to break free,

The swirling wind of ambition in her wings,

The burning passion to soar high.

But,

She is crushed,

By the social rules of

Her inferiority,

By the very own essence of the world,

Which she filled with passion.

By the very own life,

She created.

Even then,

She picks herself up,

Makes your house, a home again.

She nourishes you,

With the zeal of life.

She works tirelessly,

For her dreams,

And still makes your life comfortable.

She gives you,

The shelter of motherhood.

She is strong,

She doesn't give up,

Not on her dreams,

Never on you.

She is your mother,

Being your saviour, soothing your pain.

She is your friend,

Listening to you even when you don't say.

She is your sister,

Playfully warming up your heart.

She is your wife,

With just a smile, wearing out the tire of your day.

She is your daughter,

Who is there no matter what.

She completes you,

She completes Shiva,

She is Shakti.

The verve of creation,

The one who made life possible,

She is the woman.

By Sneha Pandey, poet and image consultant

Testament of Courage.

"Life never gives you all that you want but it gives all that you need to fulfil your wants," Maa used to tell me.

No sooner did those words flit into my head than my treacherous memories began to slide back to when I was a nine-year-old Meera.

A voice came echoed in my ears – "get into the car, fast."

It was the summer of 1992, Chandangarh village, Haryana. Gayatri, a poor farmer's wife just sat after doing her household chores when her husband Kuldip came rushing into the house, yelling at the pitch of his voice. "It's all over, we have nothing left," he said sobbing. Later Gayatri realized that he was talking about the crops, which got ruined due to lack of pest control. She knew that they already were in debts and the crops were their last hope. Kuldip decided to work in Thakur Ratan Singh's fields so that at least he would be able to feed his family. He headed immediately towards Ratan Singh's house. Meanwhile Gayatri started thinking of ways to help her husband.

It was late in the evening and there was no sign of Kuldip anywhere around. Gayatri went searching for him. Upon reaching Thakur's house, the sight chilled her to the bone. She saw her husband Kuldip being brutally beaten by Thakur's men. She ran to get him out of their clutches. When Thakur saw her coming, he asked his men to stop and leave the poor farmer lying on the floor.

She knew that Thakur was a cruel man and being the head of the Khap panchayat gave him even more authority upon the lives of these poor people. She tried helping Kuldip to get up but it was too late. Before Kuldip could utter a word, life ebbed away from him. Gayatri was more shocked than hurt. The turn of events in the last twelve hours had left her dumbfounded. She felt a wave of dizziness assail her. She screamed and cried sitting next to her dead husband but there was no one to console her.

A month had passed since Kuldip's death. Gayatri was trying hard to get the situation into her control. Her only concern wasn't feeding the family. She was thinking how she would pay back the debt. She couldn't ask Thakur for the reason behind beating her husband to death because she feared for her and her daughter's life. Though she didn't love Kuldip, but he was the only person she could rely on for herself and her nine-year-old daughter.

Even after working as a daily wage labourer at other's fields, she was hardly able to arrange for food. Paying the debt seemed an impossible task. Following the agony, the next day her door was knocked by two of Thakur's men. They told her that Thakur wanted to see her. She knew that something very bad was going to happen but she didn't dare go against Thakur. She accompanied the men back to Thakur's place.

"Come dear, sit," Thakur said upon seeing Gayatri enter his house. Gayatri was surprised by his gesture but this gave her the surety that something ominous was to happen.

"I heard that you have borrowed a big amount of money from Lakhan and have failed to pay back. I have called you here to help you. Forget about what happened to Kuldip. A son of a bitch, he was. Why are you wasting your youth, grieving for a man like him?" he said grinning.

Gayatri knew that Thakur hadn't called her to help but to take advantage of her situation. Before she could say anything, Thakur started again.

"You see, you are a young and beautiful woman and working in other's fields doesn't suit you. Why don't you work for me and in return I'll pay all your debts? You just need to please me." There was viciousness in Thakur's voice.

She could sense the filth in his intentions and rose up to leave. Thakur grabbed her arm, making it hard for her to take a move.

He just drew her face towards his and said – "You leave this house today and I'll make your life worse than hell." Gayatri knew she was trapped and there was no way she could escape.

From that day onwards, Gayatri used to visit Thakur every night to satisfy his lust; at the price of her dignity she had to save her family.

"Sacrifices are jewel to women." I've heard but which law or rule book says sacrifice your dignity to save your life. These men in the name of god or sometimes rules harass women and satisfy their male ego. Money may not buy you happiness but it surely buys you power.

This arrangement didn't work for many days. Word of Thakur's secret affair got spread and to save himself from the blame, he framed Gayatri for trying to seduce him and theft. The Khap had to do justice. They called for a meeting in the village panchayat on 28th May, 1992.

The morning of 28th May brought with it the end to one story and the start to another. Gayatri was beaten by the whole village. The Khap did justice by getting her beaten to death. I stood there watching as my whole family got destructed in a span of two months. I had nowhere to go. I couldn't save any of my parents. The next thing the Khap decided was to give me into Thakur's custody. This wasn't right I knew. He killed my parents and forced my mother into an affair. He wouldn't leave me either.

Before anyone could notice, I started to run towards the fields which led to the highway. No sooner had I started running; than I was followed by Thakur's men. I realized later that running from these men was like stepping into quicksand. I tripped and fell a few times. My clothes got all ripped and there were numerous cuts and bruises on my face and arms, but I kept running. I ran and ran till I reached the highway. I was almost about to collapse on the pavement when I saw a white Maruti 800 pull up to me. The rear passenger's side door opened and a woman commanded, 'Get into the car, fast.' The moment I got in, the car swerved away from the pavement and gathered speed. When I raised my head, I discovered a woman in her twenties, wearing a white kurta peering at me from the driver's seat. This is when my life took a 360 degree turn. This lady was Avantika Sisodiya whom I call Maa.

I learnt later about Maa. She had her own share of ups and downs. Maa was a post graduate in Literature from Delhi University and wanted to do her fellowship in the States. She was married to Mr. Abhay Sisodiya, who was the CEO of a well-known MNC. Their marriage wasn't a success but was sort of a forced relationship. Maa has always been obedient even when she wasn't supposed to be. Life is not always fair but for her it was biased in being unfair. Abhay uncle's extra marital affair was another of her concerns. She desperately wanted to break out of these clutches.

"Are you alright, dear?" she asked me with concern in her voice.

"They killed Ammo, they killed bappa." was all I could utter at that point.

Though it was just 8 a.m., Delhi was bustling with activity. This was my first day in Delhi and the beginning to a new chapter of life. We reached home at 8:30 a.m. The moment we reached home, Maa gave me her clothes to wear. I looked like one of those models who've suffered a wardrobe malfunction but that wasn't important at that time. She gave me basic first aid. Then she sat me down and asked me what had happened. I could sense the fright in the air.

"They can file a case against me. I asked you to get into the car and according to them I kidnapped you," Maa said in horror. We ought to report it to police or else they'll take you back. She discussed this with her neighbour Mrs. Sushma Sharma who worked for an NGO named "Unnati". She agreed to help and said she would introduce Maa to their head. The head was a middle-aged man. After listening to Maa, he said – "You can leave this girl here and go back to your routine life. We'll take care of her without involving the police or the Khap." There was the same vile in his voice as that of Thakur. Maa sensed the palpable tension on my face. She left saying she'd call him in the evening.

That night, as I lie in the dark, I could hear Maa tossing and turning in her bed. I knew she was thinking, there were the same thoughts as mine. All her strength had eventually come down to this bizarre predicament. She wanted to break through this. Maa got up suddenly and called her father Mr. Arjun Singh, retired Inspector general of police. She asked him if she could come over. There was a little tension on the other side. The call was terminated. She asked me to get dressed and we headed towards her parent's place in Vasant Kunj.

"You ought not keep this girl with you, she is a pack of troubles." her father said disgustedly. Maa knew that even her father wouldn't stand by her side and maybe she already was aware of this this. This man irrespective of being her father and an educated citizen didn't stand by her when she needed him the most. Why would he today?

"It's over dad, between you and me. My marriage is over and I am not listening to you anymore." Those were Maa's last words when she left her father's house.

The next I remember was Maa going to the police station and filing a case against the Khap. This followed long legal proceedings. Meanwhile Maa applied for another fellowship program. She decided to divorce her husband. Within 6 months' things worked out for us. Maa got her fellowship at the States. She won her divorce case too. The case against the Khap didn't actually work so well but thankfully Maa got my custody. On the 26th of November, 1992, we left for Indiana, USA.

Maa brought me up with love and determination. I still remember her last words, "You are my testament of courage Meera. If it would have not been for you, things would have never changed."

Maa left a letter for me with her lawyer. I couldn't dare to open it until today, but now I feel a sudden urge to open it.

My dear Meera,

If you are reading this, then I have already left this world. The disease claimed me earlier than I had expected. When you met me for the first time on that grey afternoon of 28th May, I had no idea what was to come. It is one of the paradoxes of life that the more you love yourself; the more you lose your loved ones. No amount of foresight or planning can help you survive. Life was never easy, but for you, for the love I saw in you, I changed things. It's true that individual choices are what actually matter. So, whatever you do, be yourself. Stand up for the principles you believe in. Everything else will follow.

Affectionately,

Maa

I closed the letter with tears in my eyes. Maa was a warrior, a loving mother and a persistent teacher.

I am leaving for India tonight. I am leading the project Bill Gates foundation has laid for Indian children. Sometimes it takes a trial by fire to help us know ourselves. Maa passed her tests and overcame her fears to give me a life. It's my time now. I don't believe in luck. I believe in myself. After all, life never gives you all that you want but it gives all that you need to fulfil your wants.

-   ***By Arshita Singh***

Woman

I am a woman,

Living in words of hope and sacrifice.

I am a woman,

Living in all human life with its nobility and vice.

Haunting truths of subjugation in broad daylight,

Comforting tears of loneliness in the night.

I don't need the world and its grudges against me,

But still I stand without hope for it, as it needs me.

I have been a saviour,

Of people's expectations and inane being.

I have been a murderer,

Of my own convictions and thus my zest damping.

I have been oppressed.

I have been hurt.

Stripped off dignity and pride,

Stripped off my being and me.

I have been disparaged.

I have been modified.

People control my freedom,

People control my reasons.

They turn me into a commodity,

And ask me to act in a particular way.

I am tired of being nice,

I am tired of this world,

Where everyday a woman's dreams die,

And her wings every day are cut or furled.

I am tired of the dos and the don'ts.

I am tired of the burden,

Of acting, wearing, doing, thinking in

A way, considered apt for me.

I am the reason of life,

Even then, I am the bearer of all aches and detestation.

I give, give, give and give more,

Not because I am weak,

I don't need strength from this two-faced world,

They should just know,

The burden of their deed

I am carrying.

Needs more strength to

Let go of one self,

Than they can imagine.

-   *By Sneha Pandey, poet and image consultant*

Feminism

They say feminism is a weapon,

Which women use against men,

Feminism is not against someone,

It is for women.

It is just an ideology,

Which says,

That yes!

Women are humans too.

They need freedom too,

They want to breathe in the fair air,

They want to live life,

Without so many bulwarks.

They go through the pains,

Of the pressures

Of the society,

To be a certain way.

They go through the expectations,

From the close ones,

Just because they were born,

As women.

They don't need you,

To vacate your positions in life,

They just want an understanding,

They just need empathy,

Not your criticism.

Neither your pity.

So, before pointing a finger,

Towards such women.

Know not all are the same,

Stop stereotyping,

And just try understanding,

For once,

Feel what they go through.

- *By Sneha Pandey, poet and image consultant*

Empowered

Empowered you'll be

when you develop the Strength

to say yes to your desires

to say no to things, you don't want.

No words, slogans, protests can do that

You have to feel the power within

and bring it out for everyone to see.

Empowered you'll be

when you develop the Courage

to believe in your dreams

and in your ability to fulfil those dreams.

No handholding, guidance, mentoring can do that

You have to develop the conviction within

and bring it out for everyone to see.

Empowered you'll be

when you develop the Confidence

to value yourself

and hold yourself in high esteem.

No request, reservation, appeal can do that

You have to realize your self-worth

and bring it out for everyone to see.

When you can stand up for yourself

and express your needs

When you can make bold choices

and dare to speak your heart

then, my dear lady

you will not only make it through

but make your presence felt.

Then empowered you will be

to achieve your goals

Reach for the impossible

Become a free soul

Build a brighter tomorrow.

-Dr Roopleen, Dehradun, Uttarakhand

Weak? Warrior?

Woman!!

It was a fine Monday morning when she had that intense fight with her mom and dad.

"No one loves me in this house!" her innocent heart pondered in distress.

Amyra was just in her teens when she could actually conclude who loves her, who does not.

"Why do you do this to me always?" asked Amyra to God crying in the corner. But she was unaware of life's plans that were yet to come by her way.

Days passed just like that and she encountered the guy in her own school, the one she never knew had a crush on her. And thereon life started the first chapter of its book that was yet to be opened.

Those formal talks turned into 3 a.m. chatting and even her heart did not know when she fell for him.

Talking to Kushal made her forget all her desolation and pain.

She thought life was so perfect, as it had then no regret.

"I love you Amyra," said Kushal that night, that night was something unforgettable for Amyra as she had been waiting for that day for one year. Those feelings were something beyond perfection when both of them could feel love was in the air. Slowly their love and time brought them closer. Those hugs, those kisses and those cuddles were the reason of their unexplained happiness.

"I have finally got a perfect life!" sighed Amyra. But then life giggled in the corner for she could never sense Kushal's exaggerated manipulative mind. Slowly things changed and Kushal's care and love turned into dominance and possessiveness. She was no longer his love but only an obsession.

She never expected that the kisses and cuddles would one day turn into a struggle.

Her heart got hurt for the first time when Kushal insulted her by abusing her. Those lips which once opened for love only had abuses pouring out of them. But Amyra was so much in love with Kushal that she excused him and continued her life with him. Poor Amyra, that was the biggest mistake of her life as she never knew that forgiveness would be considered as her weakness.

Amyra was a fun loving, daddy's girl, pampered with extreme love which she hadn't realised in time. She couldn't see that her life was more carefree and perfect before Kushal had come. But that monster wanted something else completely. Abuse was then the only reaction to every single thing which was done against Kushal's wish. Her life had become just like a time table which was not at all possible for a human to follow. But Amyra tried. She managed to do that as she had no other option because she was so much afraid to let any of her family members get to know about them. So she lived a life that Kushal wanted.

"Being a girl there are some limits you should stay in. You should not raise you pitch of voice. You should not hang out with anyone after 6 p.m. You should not make male friends. You should dress like a girl!" quoted Kushal.

And the moment that timetable was disregarded, she was already prepared to bear the agony of that savage. Yes! You read it right. That beast had then deteriorated to such a level of savagery that he started beating her like a heartless monster even on her smallest mistakes. She was not even allowed to choose the professional course for her career. "You are a girl. You don't need to set a future as you are going to be a housewife only", said Kushal.

Every girl has a dream of getting proposed by a boy on his knees. Amyra was no different but her destiny definitely was! She was the one who had to go down every time on her knees to plead to Kushal, "Please forgive me. Please don't hit me, it hurts!"

Abused, tortured and beaten like a slave, apologies were made but he didn't behave.

Amyra was tortured in every possible way. Though physical marks of his evilness disappeared in few days but those marks of fear and helplessness got engraved on her heart which were nowhere easy to get rid of.

Those mental tortures, those abuses, those physical pains and that manipulative mind of Kushal! Amyra was viciously trapped in her own life.

Nights were full of tears and days were full of fears.

She was tired of every torture, unlucky Amyra had no supporter!

She was tough enough to sustain that pressure for three damn years, but wasn't brave enough to tell anyone what she was going through. No part of her body was left untouched by that monster. She was touched not by love but only by discourtesy and anger.

"I want to die!" cried Amyra to God, for she tried to commit suicide thrice. That time also God had planned something else for her.

She was completely shattered and dejected of her life. Finally, she gathered all her nerves and called up her sister and said, "Radhika please save me from that devil. He beats me very harshly. I need you help!" and the phone was disconnected.

Radhika felt little chaotic at what she heard. That very moment she left all her work and went to Amyra's place to figure out the matter. Tears rolled down from their eyes as Amyra revealed her pain to Radhika. From one's eyes those were the tears of torment and from other's were the tears of commiseration.

"Hey sweetheart! Tell your eyes to hold on those tears. Those days have ended now!" consoled Radhika.

"Do not ever forget that if a woman can create this world then she has the power to destroy it too!" she inspired Amyra.

"But didi, I am afraid of him...", feared Amyra.

"Afraid of what Amyra? That coward wretch who cannot see you happy or successful because he knows you are more talented than him? You are in no way less than him and you know this thing very well." Radhika again motivated her.

"What should I do then?"

"Nothing much! You just need to believe in yourself and show him what you actually are..."

After those words from Radhika, Amyra had a bunch of questions revolving around in her mind. "Why did all that happen? How could I suffer so much at the hands of that monster? Was it all my mistake? Am I really not strong?" She was all puzzled and the only answer she got to all the questions was, "It all happened because I let him do that to me. It was my mistake that being strong enough I didn't take a stand!"

Things between them changed after that. Amyra refused to meet Kushal whenever he wanted to meet her. She started talking to him rudely. And the day came when they met after so many days and Kushal was unaware of whatever was going to happen to him that day. Amyra was all prepared mentally to face him bravely. When he tried to slap her, she clenched his hand and smacked him with all her anger. And the most amusing part was that all four fingers of her hand could be clearly seen on his cheek!

"Enough is enough Kushal! I loved you, and that doesn't mean I owe you anything or you own me," retorted Amyra.

"And yes, you were talking about my limits! Who are you to decide my limits? That was not my limit that I stayed quiet but it was my love and respect for you which a person like you does not deserve at all. And you should be thankful to me that I didn't raise my voice much before and helped you maintain your futile male ego!" she yelled.

No other reaction of Amyra could be better than taking a stand for her self-respect. Amyra had then realised that it was not 'she' who was weak but Kushal's love which had made her weak. It required her to take a stand just once even much before that to set everything at right place. She could feel that deep inside her was a brave Amyra who was curbed and stuck in a dark corner.

That day she decided to live a life of her own and follow her dreams only. She focussed only on her goals to be a happy and successful woman.

Years passed and now she is the CEO of a reputed Multi-National Company.

So! What are the limits of a woman?

Is she the one whose goals are to be hurled away, or the one born to rule this world?

No one is born to be a slave and of course 'gender' is never a measurement of anyone's abilities or limits.

And I feel pity on those men who think raising their voice or hands on a woman adds an 'honour' to their so called male ego.

We women are the warriors born to conquer this world!

FOR A WOMAN,

EVEN THE SKY IS NOT THE LIMIT!

SHE IS BORN TO FLY AND RISE ABOVE ALL

FOR THE THUNDERSTORM INSIDE HER CAN OBLITERATE YOU!

- *By Sonal Jain*

Only if –

Only if you people would have let me survive,

And not so brutally you would have taken my life.

I would have done all that is done by your beloved son,

And with my innocence and smile, your hearts I would have won.

I swear I would have never asked for any toy,

And also would never have been less than a boy.

Even though not white, I was considered grey,

But here in heaven, for you dad, I would forever pray.

If family's RESPECT is what my birth would have kept at stake,

This little angel of yours is even ready to be your hidden mistake.

-    *By Sana Sheikh*

The changing face of feminism

Feminism, thy name is beauty

Thy name is courage,

Thy name is trust,

Thy name is love.

Then why does everybody call it only females' duty?

Instead, participation of men will make this movement, more sacred, more strong and more impactful.

Today, the country is developing. The people are developing but what is not developing is the mind-set of few people, who are still in a dilemma whether women are equal or not. In fact, there are some women too who have become extra sensitive, taking advantage of their gender, i.e. of being women.

According to me, feminism is not just about the impartial treatment given to women. But Feminism is the movement which sees both the genders equally. There's no stamp on women that they are inferior to men and similarly Lord has never told that men are superior to women. Then why the bias? Just because the mind-set of few narrow-minded people has grown like a weed which is affecting the whole crop of mankind. And it's really essential to burn this weed right away otherwise who knows who and what will be affected?

It also refers to the uplift-ment of the women of the weaker sections of the society so that they can also earn a name for themselves and prove their worth to the society. But in the process we should take care not to superimpose our thoughts on any other person. Feminism makes a person perseverant, vigilant, concerned, patient, sensitive, emotional and respectful to everyone's point of view.

There are some so called 'educated men' in the society who consider their educated wives to be just their caretakers and not their partners, which really exposes their pervert character. They are raising their voice against the impartial treatment given to women, but as soon as they enter their house, they get angry if they aren't served water by their wives. Is this education? Or is this real support?

This is just hypocrisy, mere a show off to raise their standard in the society. Why they never feel guilty of this diplomatic behaviour? How are they able to face themselves in the mirror, when they aren't true to themselves too? I hate these 'educated people'. I can't stand these people.

However, there are others also who are really supporting the females in the real sense. They are having no objection regarding women's education, her dressing sense, her career or her way of handling situations. Hats off to these Real Men.

There are many theories regarding feminism doing the rounds and people are running around them. But does this really matter? Yes, it does matter. After all, it educates us, makes us aware about the various situations which people face, enlightens us about the different mind-sets. But what matters in the end is the implication of the particular Feminist Movement.

Definitely, to survive today's complex lifestyle and to progress further in one's life, the thin line between partial vs impartial treatment, respect vs disrespect, love vs insult and most importantly abiding the rules wishfully vs forcefully should be respected and taken care of.

The fact is that there is presence of male in the society because of a female.

People should realize,

from FEMALE only we get MALE.

If no FEMALE, no MALE

Thus the practice of female foeticide, wherever present in the society should be eradicated by one and all. From birth itself, both the genders should be treated with same love, care and nourishment. Along with the girls of the house, the boys should also be told to be in their limits. Then hopefully, one day we can have an impartial India.

Thus, respect one and all

As men and women are just the seeds of that superpower,

Who have their own individuality,

Their own freedom and

Their own expression

Let us nurture them according to their needs

So as to get an orchard just like heaven.

Justification will be done

Only if

On every lip, there's an "Amen"

Whenever there's a birth of any man or woman

- *By Ruchika Rastogi*

The woman she knew, the story she did not.

Part 1

Confused, alarmed, dejected she was always;

Especially when she saw different men pass her ways,

From her mother's room every day,

Through the window voices she heard, where she aimlessly lay.

The sounds emanating inside the room horrified her,

Followed by the angry jibes and slurs.

A living subject of loneliness, contempt and ridicule she had become.

She was nice and sweet to everyone, but no one allowed her in their frame.

Every day she wondered, what was her mistake,

Why was she punished so badly by her fate?

Alienated by the society, despised by her own mother.

With no one to hold on to, life had become a living purgatory for her.

It was then that she desired to know the real story

Which was harsh and gory.

The deed she knew, the story she did not.

The woman she knew, the story she did not.

Part 2

There she was sitting crouched, along with ten different girls,

In a tiny room, not allowed to utter a word.

Sold to a brothel owner like a cheap object.

She had merely became a tool in their hands.

Overwhelmed by a sense of panic and fear,

Stripped of her independence, her rights over her body,

Her rights over her life, but no one seemed to care.

She tried to defy their orders and escape,

But she failed and became the subject of grievous abuse and rape.

She was forced to lead the life of a sex slave.

She had no money and hence absconding was not a way.

Every night behind the hordes of makeup, was a terrifying plight of a woman

Who was berated lower than a human.

It was during those days an illegitimate child took birth,

Which she had to bring up on her own in this filth and dirt.

Finally, she planned and ran away with the child,

But there was no job for survival that she could find.

She cursed the little one with all the expletives and with anger she went berserk

Finding the child responsible for her return to her old work.

Part 3

Till when will these women suffer?

Till when will this dance of horror continue and the law will not interrupt?

How many women and children do we want to kill

Every day by this evil?

The silence needs to be broken

The power needs to be shaken

Only then there will be change that we desire.

A change that we aspire.

- *By Arpita Gupta*

Expulsion

It was a village. Full of greenery and marked by the unity of its residents. One among those living there was Rehan. He lived with his daughter, Shabana, in a poorly made house. His wife had already passed away. Needless to say, life was hard for them. Despite that, Shabana had a deep desire to learn. Her mother had often told her that lack of education was the cause of poverty. Shabana often wondered if the case was the reverse for them. Mustering up courage one day, she asked her father about it.

"I will educate you, no matter what difficulties come," Rehan assured her.

Little was he aware of the bout of difficulties ahead, which began too soon for Rehan to handle. The village had a higher secondary school, but the students allowed there were only boys. Shabana was about to pass high school already. The village head's daughter, Zoya, was her classmate and friend. Shabana asked her if she was going for higher education. "How can I? You know we are supposed to handle the household. Abbu would say, 'What will you do by studying further? As much you have studied is more than enough. We were generous to spend that much on your unnecessary education.'"

"But, I want to study further!" Shabana insisted.

"Good. If you attend, I will come with you to the school too," said Zoya, adding softly, "if Abbu allows."

When she went home, Shabana informed Rehan of the talk between her and Zoya. Rehan knew that the village head would never allow girls in the school. He might have to face the village head due to his daughter's words and probable actions.

The very next morning, an assembly of villagers were called. Rehan was greeted by a man on his door, and was informed that he had been called with his daughter to the assembly. This was what Rehan had feared.

"Your daughter!" the village head began, "How dare she! She tried to brainwash my girl. Who put the idea of further education into her little head? Rehan! Have you not taught her any manners? Will she attend classes further, in spite of being a girl?"

"But, Maalik, it is her choice. She wants to study."

"Silence!" the village head's voice roared. "It is my village. The higher school is for the boys only. If your daughter wants to study more, and if you want to be a slave to her, leave my village. Out, I say!"

All the villagers agreed to the head's decision and scorned Rehan for bowing down to his daughter's whims. He was given a day to decide whether he would let Shabana follow her dreams, or stay in the village following the village head's orthodox views. When he stepped inside the house, the same thoughts cluttered his mind. He decided to go out for a walk, hoping to learn the answer to his troubled thoughts.

When he returned home that evening, Rehan had his answer waiting. He came face to face with the mentality prevailing in the village. He was shocked when he heard that Zoya had been beaten badly by the village head, and her quest of education had been proved futile, just as her name, and soul. Even her mother was not spared, who tried to protect her from her father's angry hands. While Shabana had done the unacceptable, she had topped the village school. Rehan's thoughts were no longer troubled. He had come to his decision.

"Pack up our belongings," Rehan instructed Shabana, "we are leaving tomorrow." Rehan did not know where he would go, or how he would pay for Shabana's education. He was just an unskilled labourer. But his decision was firm, and Shabana's desire was compelling.

The next day they left, and the village head seemed too happy about it. So did the villagers. After all, the village was proud of the unity of its residents. They all felt good to have set an example by expelling the ones who tried to break the norms they took pride in.

Years passed.

No one seemed to remember Rehan and his daughter. No one thought that they must have gone to a city, spent hungry nights, survived without shelter, and endured so much, just for the sake of education. No one but Zoya. She was married now, as her father thought that early marriage was the key to end all the problems caused to him by his daughter. Zoya often thought about Shabana, who used to tell her that she was lucky to be the village head's daughter. She had doubts on those words earlier, but now, she believed that those words were false.

A few months later, Zoya visited her father's place. She found it strange, that the very house that seemed to be hers, had turned to be her 'father's place', soon after she was married. She was pregnant for the third time, and her mother was supposed to be by her side. But how Zoya longed for her childhood friend! She wished that Shabana could be with her, by her side, and helped her endure all the pain. Much of which she carried in her heart. She tried to recollect Shabana's face. It seemed so tough!

Suddenly, she felt pain. It seemed to be killing her. She screamed out, and fell unconscious. When she woke up, she found herself in the village hospital. Her father was screaming at the doctor. "I don't know how you treat her. Nothing must happen to the child. I want a grandson!"

"Please understand," the village doctor tried to calm him, "it is a case for a lady doctor. I can't handle such a case."

"What? A lady doctor?" the village head seemed surprised. He had never heard of a lady doctor. Zoya had fainted again.

Someone suggested taking her to a city. "At least the child will be saved."

Hours later, Zoya regained consciousness. She no longer felt any pain. But this was a different hospital, and there were lots of unrecognised faces. Her father was regretting over denying education to girls in his village, and complaining about how he had to come to the city for his grandchild's sake. Zoya was greeted by a lady doctor, who sat beside her, and handed her the baby. Zoya looked at her smile. Somehow it seemed so familiar. And so did the name on the white coat.

"Dr. Shabana," it read.

- *By Ayush Ashish*

Afterglow

Face your fears,

Let your light shine.

Be stubborn, girl,

Hold your head high!!

Let the wars wage on,

Be your own knight in shining armour.

Slay all the dragons,

Girl, wait for no man with fake ardour!!

Be a princess, if you want,

Or, be a general in a war.

Girl, let no one stray you,

Be filled with light in your core!!

Be a homemaker, if you want,

Or, be a professional with a job.

Girl, let your dreams be the judge of your wants,

Not people who forever taunt!!

Be an artist, who paints,

Or a discoverer who stakes claim.

Don't let prejudices bind you,

Girl, be the one to follow your aim!!

Wear a bikini, if you want,

Or, wear a gown with pouf.

Girl, leave yourself, be free of fear,

Let, only God be the judge of your account!!

Be the one with a wild spirit,

Or, the mellow one with a novel and coffee in tow.

Girl, become any one you want,

Just, enjoy the life you've found!!

Don't care, if you're dark or as white as milk,

Don't worry about the moles or marks on your skin.

Girl, let no groom force you to change who you are,

Because, you're worthy enough to not need the support of their kin!!

Don't care, if you're as fat as a bun,

Or as thin as a stick.

Don't let people degrade you,

Girl, be comfortable in your own skin!!

Girl, the world around will fade,

People mixing within shadows.

Be the one to resurrect you,

Bestow on yourself the afterglow!!

- *By Fatma Naqvi*

You go, girl!

Congrats to you girl,

As you managed to take birth in this whirl.

Feel lucky as you were given a chance to live,

But don't feel bad if your birth was a furtive,

To live in this world one needs a lot of courage,

As for you, the motive is to save your image.

Everyone told you to dress up according to the culture,

As outside there are many men, resting their eyes on you, like a vulture.

Wearing a short dress is strictly prohibited,

As according to many,it makes your image blighted.

Be conscious to hide your bra strap,

As these things are responsible for any mishap,

Wear clothes which hide your belly,

A girl's character is decided by the length of dress above the knee,

How strange equality it is!

No matter, you wear a burkha or a saree you drape,

No matter you are 10 or 70, you still can get raped.

Mentality prevalent is, whatever happens with you is just because of the exposure,

It was reminded to you, that with men not to get closer.

Still girl, don't get afraid, come out of the walls,

Do such a thing that raises up squalls.

Do what you want, dress up in your own way,

And always be courageous, to say yea or nay.

By Nandini Saxena

My Verdict

I've always heard that society is always fair. Or at least that was what I was made to believe since I was a kid. I always wanted to be a fashion-model. I took part in most of the contests in my school and won. Everyone told me that I was made for it. I'm 22 now. I've been a feminist for five years. You might be wondering why I haven't chosen modelling. Well then, here lies the reason.

I was seventeen when my only sister, Kashvi, who is elder to me, got engaged to a local guy. Ours was a small town so the guy and his family were an acquaintance. Kashvi was 24, which means that the pressure of marriage was a lot. Kashvi was a topper and wanted to continue studying but my parents couldn't afford it as it was something that could be done only at the expense of her image in the society. She agreed to marry the guy whom my parents thought was right for her.

The wedding was in two months. It was going to be a typical Indian wedding, arranged and supervised by the elders. Ours was a middle-class family and the budget for the wedding was already over our heads. But the groom's family kept insisting on an extravagant one because a simple one would badly impact their 'so-called' reputation in the town. My parents were going to spend all their savings. I offered them all the money I had collected by winning prizes or saving in my own little ways; but they wouldn't accept it.

Everything was going fine. It was hard, but it was fine as long as it meant Kashvi would lead a happy life ahead. The wedding was to be held in fifteen days. Kashvi was pretending to be happy but I knew she was not. A part of her still craved the education-life. Oh, how she loved studying! I was praying for the smile on my parents' face to last long and for nothing to jinx it. That's when the boy's family dropped the bomb.

They visited our home over tea when the to-be-groom's father asked, "So, how much is it going to be?" I was in the next room, listening.

At first my parents, obviously, had no clue what he was talking about. "I'm not sure I follow you, Samdhee Saab," my Dad replied.

"Don't act. You know I'm talking about the dowry." He smirked.

"But-" Dad's voice cracked. "You didn't talk about this when we fixed the wedding."

"Ha-ha. Isn't it obvious, Raam ji? You can't get your girl married without dowry!" he said, letting out a small laugh.

My parents were silent. It broke me to see them like that so I walked into the living room and without thinking twice I said, "It's illegal. I'll report you!" I didn't regret it. The man shot me a nasty look and before I could say anything, my Mom asked me to go inside and not to get involved in the elders' talks. I went in. I could hear my parents apologizing to my sister's future father-in-law. I didn't know what to do. The man and his wife left after half an hour.

 Mom came into my room, and said, "Why did you do that? Don't you want your sister to get married?"

I was shocked. "But Maa, they were asking for dowry!"

"We have to give them what they ask. We can't risk calling the wedding off. It is frowned upon in the society!" She answered. I remained quiet, I didn't want to bother them more than they already were.

Later that day I heard my Mom crying. Dad was trying to comfort her. He couldn't afford or manage to pay the dowry. We had already spent too much on the wedding expenses.

"We've to get through this. I can't see you like this. We've already spent so much, a little more can't hurt."

"We can't afford ninety thousand rupees!" my Mom replied, half crying.

"We can take a collateral loan on our house. We could sell the little land; it's not of much use to us." My Dad's voice rasped. I couldn't bear it.

I was trying to listen when Kashvi asked me what had happened. I couldn't lie to her. I tried but failed. She could easily tell when I was lying. When I told her everything she broke down. She couldn't control herself.

"I'm such a burden to them. I can't do this anymore. I don't want to marry!"

I tried to calm her. But it was of no use. She went to bed weeping terribly. I did the same. I had a contest the next day. I needed sleep.

The next morning, I went to the city centre for the contest. I was disturbed the whole time. My designer was very worried about me as I had been lost in my own thoughts. I went back home, sulking. The worse was to come. People were gathered outside my house. Loud wails were coming from inside. I parted to make my way through the crowd and went in. I collapsed and fell to the floor when I saw what it was all about.

Kashvi.

She had committed suicide. She had taken some unsafe pills when my parents had gone out. My vision was going black. My world collapsed. Tears gushed out and all I was feeling was emptiness and the loss of purpose. Everything followed. The services, the sympathies, everything! Was this why she had to get married? What she did was wrong, but did she have a choice?

If this is how the society is fair, I call quit. That day, I knew what I wanted to become. A feminist. If Kashvi would want something, it would be this. No other girl should have to face this horrendous fate.

I want to work for what I believe in. Rights for girls. I see a purpose in feminism. This is what I want to strive for. This is it. I decided that day, that there would be no looking back. And here I am today, talking to you beautiful people out there. I hope you approve of this. We are the feminists. There is no weaker gender. This is what we believe in.

-   *By Kruthika Reddy*

Woman - raped???

You broke into her body,
Thinking you have won over her,
Fulfilling your hedonistic fantasies.
Yes.
You did.
Maybe for an hour or a day.
But then she hasn't succumbed to those injuries.
The scars that remain,
Shall become talismans of her struggles for survival.
Her audacity to live in a world that has failed her.
True.
People stare, talk and pass snide comments,
And yet, her eyes blaze with a fire.
Vengeance that shall one day crumble your so called manliness,
Karma shall get back to you.
But she will keep living, despite the odds,
Ordeals making her an epitome of strength and valour,
She isn't a museum of past turmoil.
Today she rises from the mangled remains of her body,
Purged and purified by the flames that course through her veins.
She is that unsung hero,
A fresh blossom of another spring.
You were grossly wrong when you thought you had trampled her
in winter's chill.
For she is perennial,
Demons in her mind she has tamed,
And no matter how hard you try,
Her unchained spirit you can never claim.
A woman raped
Isn't a victim.
She is power – unleashed,
Her voice resounding forever.
In this so called world of patriarchy
She is the Queen...

-    *By Samrudhi Dash*

Yes! She is a woman.

A soul so hard and a heart of gold.

A personality in various situation it can mould...

Plays different roles at the same time...

Makes life beautiful just as a rhyme...

Does not leave behind a single stone unturned...

No power can make her feel all threatened...

She knows how to take whatever she wants...

With all her might, her beauty she flaunts...

Does not commit a crime but takes in all the blames...

Without any reason she is asked to burn in the flames...

Killed when she is born she continues to leave her legacy...

She shows it strong but cries in privacy...

She does not let anyone let her down...

She is what makes SHE, the most powerful pronoun...

It is her determination that has broken all the chains...

It is her dedication that has given her this name...

She is the living Goddess, teaching us hard work with compassion...

She is the one who shows the true meaning of passion...

Just by existing, she puts up a beautiful omen...

Yes, we are proud that she is a woman!

- *By Simran Sharma*

Liberated

Born strong.
The ladies, men admire, I've heard,
Would shudder at a wicked word.
Out of the ash
I desperately want to scream

Out of the forest I come with my flowers, singing, all alone.
The planet goes on being round.

I may shoot with words,
I may cut with eyes,
I may kill with hatefulness,
But still, like air, I'll rise.

And wrap around
just like a shawl,
Qualified to live
It is better to speak
than wait for moments that
validate me as a woman.

- *By Bhooma Bhagat*

Woman: The Diamond Dust

She may boil in the bowl of rice all day,

But she does not get evaporated,

When you increase the heat.

She remains in each grain of rice,

Becoming softer, whiter, better.

You may swallow her up

And she becomes your vitamins.

That is what she is,

A woman who boils in the pan,

Of your tumultuous life.

Sometimes beaten, sometimes eaten,

But ultimately, she nourishes your soul.

She bears your part, begets your blood,

And grants you the first right,

To her love-showering lap and bosom.

Her forehead becomes the shield,

In times of scandalous catastrophes;

And her sari wraps and protects

Your head from the menace of the floods.

She boils and feeds your belly

With the syrup of love in drought.

She is a woman,

The diamond dust.

- *By Bandana Kar*

The girl next door

To and for,

Every girl next door...

Yes, you are a common girl, yet special.

Yes, you may have played cricket on the streets even with boys.

Yes, you may have climbed up a tree to get a fruit or just for fun.

Yes, you may have tried to dress up in your mother's saree.

Yes, you may have been waiting to go on a solo trip.

Yes, you may have more male friends than female; even Lord Krishna had more female friends.

Yes, you may have been told not todo this or that.

Yes, you may have thought to run away from home.

Yes, you may have found yourself unsafe on roads; trust me even males are not safe.

You may have hated all the boys just because of a few.

You may have cried on your pillow at night; even boys do that.

Yes, you may have been frustrated at times for the restrictions placed on you; even boys are.

Yes, you may have wished you were a boy; don't know about boys in this case.

Yes, you may be living with a dream of changing the world.

Yes, you may have lots and lots of thoughts troubling you in your head.

And lots more…

But trust me even boys face almost all that.

Come out of your thoughts, bring them to action.

Live your life and your dreams.

Respect a person and not a gender.

Don't run to seek out sympathy, run to earn respect.

Be the cause of smile of many.

Be the source of inspiration for many.

Spread love and ignore hatred, it will soon melt and vanish away.

Remember that you may be just a Girl Next Door but you can always become The Girl that every girl next door wants to be…

-By Aarohy Kapoor

For I am a woman?

I cry in agony,

For this world gives me pain.

My tears have dried up,

As the World tortures me so much.

I wake up early before the morning glow,

And sleep when the rest are in their dreams.

I carry the heavy burdens of life,

While others are enjoying their life.

Why this torturous life for me?

…. FOR I AM A WOMAN????

I cook delicious meals,

And clean the household,

For my family to remain content.

I discipline the cute infants,

And nurture the lovely children,

For our family to prosper.

I play with the naughty ones,

And joke with the smiling ones,

For them to become strong and smart.

I plan the meetings and the picnics,

For all to benefit and be merry.

I fight with the arrogant neighbours,

To bring peace and happiness to my family.

Yet the world around me,

Just ignores me so much!

Why this torturous life for me?

.... FOR I AM A WOMAN????

The poor gleam of the lantern,

Is proof of my ambitious zeal,

To educate myself and prosper.

The long hours of the night,

Subjects me to wrinkles and black eyes,

Yet, I do not complain at all.

When the stage is set for honours,

My name doesn't appear anywhere,

For I am just a frail old woman.

Why this torturous life for me?

.... FOR I AM A WOMAN????

-

- *By Shabbirhusein K Jamnagerwalla*

Feminism

The seed of feminism has started growing

Vision is clear but the destination is far

It's not easy to change old thinking

Your opinions have made a difference

Raise your voice so all can hear

Old philosophies are soon going to rumple

New era with new light of feminism

Equal rights with no more criticism

Oh my dear, please come out

Let the world, know of your worth

Discover your path, make your own way

Lead your life with a big dream

Don't let anyone hold you back

Make everyone realize that you can sack

Much more intelligent with a sense of poise

Strong enough to be independent with all new principles

Your wisdom can never prove wrong

Girls, you need to know the faces of world

Not everyone is there with you all

My ideologies different from yours

Have turned sweet pie into sour curd

You are alone in the fight of justice

Rest are there for giving sympathy

The tiny bud has blossomed from the shoot

Small feet now need bigger boots

Slowly but definitely the change will come

Arrived is stage where everyone can love

Small steps taken were always right

Fire of feminism is flying as kite

The day shines, the will is mine

Let the kite fly high in the sky

- *By Suman Gupta*

I am an ocean

I am an Ocean,
lukewarm, floating there are

women in me that are willing to breathe

I wait, silently to seep into something meaningful
I may not be perfect but I am beautiful for all the resilience
I carry in my waves.
Shedding. Soaking. Swelling.
Love is out of
my atmosphere.
Some days I spill in afternoons

the women I
am trying to be.
blue,sad, yours.
There is a fire that will
burn brighter,
this is all I feel.
To the women in me that were
slaughtered, regarded to be low and
unequal.
To the women in me it was
said that she did not belong here.
To the women in me that couldn't
speak when softer, but being soft
is also strong,never did you
know that.
You do not know all the
power, that I am a living massacre, Kali, Durga
and mother Mary.
Ask me how I carry the

oceans inside me.
And I only taste of heart break and difficulty to you.

- *By Deepali Gupta*

The voice of an Ironman

I stand tall and firm
Not more than 5'3"
Intimidating enough?
Or maybe not!

My cheeks fall down,
As the gravity pulls.
My stomach flows out,
Filled with carbs full.

I am brown so is my skin,
Not so fair; nor too dark.
My eyes aren't light-
Like oceans and stars.

I stand with a soul,
As pure as the Ganges.
Dedicating myself;
To the duties I hold.

But on the red days-

My virtue is put to test.

They call me impure and

Forbid me for seven days.

Yet, I stand in the morning,

Looking at the door,

To guard it like

The man in uniform.

I fight the monsters,

Under all their beds.

Until I am sure,

My eyes won't blink.

I stand in my workplace,

Fulfilling all my roles.

While eggs and cutlets await

The tummies they are for.

I look for them when

IronMan they call,

I reach out for them,

And solve all the errors.

Simplest are my duties,

And so are my chores.

Be in my place someday,

Then will you learn.

A lady is not just a lady,

Neither inferior, nor superior.

Stands facing the world,

To fight and live like human'.

- ***By Ummesalma Rampurwala***

Deepa's Dream

"How dare you? Don't come near me. How could you cheat me... you liar...you bitch...I don't have any words in my stock for you, unchaste woman!"

His physical slap didn't pain more than his revile. Prateek darted out of the room but Deepa didn't care to call him back. She was neither sorry for the deed nor for the baby who was now sleeping on the cot next to her bed. She collected herself and advanced towards the cot. Her sweet little one was in deep slumber. She bent down and gave a soft kiss on her forehead. The baby smiled in her dream.

Two years ago the situation of Deepa's home-

Prateek returned from his office tour on the day of their fourth marriage anniversary. He worked as a software engineer for a reputed foreign company and occasionally went on foreign tours. He didn't have much time to spend with his wife but he claimed to love her madly.

But this time he seemed cold to Deepa.

They were meeting for the first time after her operation. Deepa had been suffering with severe pain in her left breast. She was so busy juggling things between her home and her job that she didn't pay any attention to it until the situation got worse.

Prateek was out of the city and she didn't have anyone to consult regarding her situation. Her mother wasn't strong enough to handle the crisis. After passing two sleepless nights she thought of sharing the matter with her colleague, Tina Parikh. She asked her immediately to consult a gynaecologist.

Tina proved to be a good friend more than just a colleague. She took her to a renowned doctor Mrs. Palkiwala. Deepa explained all her problem and then poured out her fear "Will the breast be removed?"

The doctor calmly said "Don't worry dear, let me check you first."

But Deepa couldn't stop herself from worrying. She couldn't understand how her body would look like if one of her breast wasn't there. She couldn't understand how she would accept the fact. And the other fear lurking in her mind was - How would Prateek react?

She went through many tests after which she was asked to undergo a breast surgery immediately. This was a vital decision. How could she take it without Prateek's consent? Mrs. Palkiwala warned her not to be late else it could become more serious.

Deepa felt dizzy hearing the doctor but she had to be strong too. After Tina left her at her home she called Prateek. He wasn't busy in a meeting, so he received the call, "Hello dear, how are you?"

Her voice was faltering. She explained everything to him. He answered in a voice warmer than she had expected.

"Oh, yes darling, you must undergo the operation immediately. I want to talk to the doctor myself. Please give me the number. Have you asked your sister Rupa to come and stay with you for a few days? It'll be great help. In the meantime, I'll try to arrange my return ticket. I have to talk to my seniors too!" Deepa got some mental support and was much stronger when she underwent the operation.

Rupa could spare a week from her busy schedule to look after her elder sister. But Prateek didn't return from his tour. He only talked over the phone and finished his duty. Rupa returned to her place immediately after the doctor removed the bandage and declared that all was fine. Deepa had to take rest and also go ahead with radiotherapy.

Deepa was left all alone to discover a new situation in the old place. That was the day when she first met her reflection in the mirror after that unwanted yet extremely important operation. She looked at herself and felt ugly and disheartened.

Her mind was in turmoil. Hot tears flowed down her cheeks and she hit her fists on the wall in a futile attempt to change the reality. Prateek returned after a month. He repented that he couldn't come earlier when she was in need. He decided to dine out to celebrate their anniversary.

Later at night on bed he took her in his tight embrace. She was happy, excited in his arms and a bit relaxed from the fear that moved in her mind. His love making was getting wild when he pulled off the last piece of cloth from her body. Suddenly his mood changed. He made her stand and had a long look at her. His look made Deepa feel like standing nude in front of public.

He turned away his face and said, "I'm tired and need rest. Put on your clothes and go to sleep." Deepa was deeply hurt with this indignity. How could Prateek act so insensitively? She glanced at him and slipped away to the other room with her night dress.

After that night their beds were separated and an invisible wall stood between them. Prateek told her that though it was important for her to undergo such a dangerous operation but he couldn't accept her that way. He said that he wouldn't ask her to leave the house but at the same time she couldn't expect any favour from him.

Deepa felt dejected but reality stood facing her. She didn't wish to live with a man who didn't love her anymore. She left his house and settled in a paid apartment near her office. She took a decision too. She would have a child of her own and bring it up without any help from any male. She could never forget how her husband behaved with her when she was in need of his support. She decided to be a single mother.

She consulted Mrs. Palkiwala and discussed regarding her need. She took the necessary steps told by the doctor to be a mother.

She smiled when she saw Prateek leave. She had won over him. She would never let him know that Sukanya came into the world through in vitro fertilization. She is only hers and no one else's.

-   ***By Sonali Basu***

Queens in armour

I am the queen
My Lord, Coined me the Queen

I am Razia, the fighter
I am Ayesha, the scholar
I am Khadija, the merchant
I am Khawlah, the activist
I am Nusayba, the warrior
I am the mystic, the Rabia
I am the martyr, the Zaynab
I am the fighter, the Sura

Come on, if you hit me,
I have the armour
Yes, I cover,
Because I am blessed
With aesthetic
Beautiful body,
For which
I have seen dynasties fight
From me were born you
My womb
My lap
My fruits
That yielded you.
Love me.
But sorry if you don't
I also have the light
That'll extinct you
I am my father's pride
My husband's bride
Separation is a curse

For you and me
Let me fly away
In freedom
For my Lord
Gave me the right
Don't mistake my ability
By my Veil
I'm a princess
In real
I am a
Clan tigress
Co-dependant
Beware!!
I am armed by a sword
And I should be loved by all!!

\- *By Ashi Kalim*

I am sorry to be born

I am sorry
    For myself
I was kicked
   Away from heaven
To this immortal world
   Where
   Seasons come
Leaves drop dead
   Life and death
Inevitable

   Yes, I am sorry
   For myself
I hide from your
   Gazing eyes
That craves for my
   Well arched body
The fruits God gave me
   Nourishes your child

But Yes, I am sorry
   You can't hear
  Me cry
For I am bound
By chains of duties
   Bound to menfolk
   Father, Brother
   Or be it Son
Come relieve Me
From the elixirs
Of Hell on Earth

O! Menfolk, folklore
    I yearn
    I plead
    Mercy
I am a burning pyre
    Neither I burn
    Nor I turn ash
Give me a new life
And, yes,again
    I am sorry
    To be Born
As a FRAGILE FELINE!!!

-    *By Ashi Kalim*

I am born again....

Yes, I am born again
   The hue and cry
   Eyes all dry
I plead you
Please welcome me
To this mesmerizing
     world
Mother, why are you sad
   See I am not bad
   I feel the pain that
      You had
I'll clad you
With comfort
    And Love
    See.....
I won't die brutal
Like NIRBHAYA
To die young
NOR AS BILKEES
NOR AS AYUSHI
I was burnt as
Witches and Whores
I was born folklore
But still
I am the Laxmi Bai
See I am this warrior
A fighter
I am Kalpana
I am Malala
I am Sania
I am Teresa
I am the Light
That'll rule your world!!

I plead to you
Please welcome me....

- *By Ashi Kalim*

64 cups of elixir

He started to masturbate;
They said "It was because 'He' has desires".
Her menstrual cycle started;
They started their own cycle of blasphemy.
Storm resided in both the bodies.
One was becoming malignant;
While the other was becoming benign.
They forgot that before birth pain crawls in the body.
Blasphemy was just a start;
It was just a pain covering a birth.
Like molten lava forms the surface of volcano;
To kill someone trigger needs to be pressed;
A watch ends when time crosses the limit;
But her limit travelled beyond the limit;
With a never ending 'watch' her hunt started;
A proper warm hearted hunt;
Unlike the cold hearted murder of a blasphemous being;
On the road her cycle started;
But now her DNA faced the truth;
The strand stopped their trembling.
Bonds are much stronger;
The whole stage belonged to them;
To reveal what is truly theirs;
They now demanded criticism on their hunt;
Unlike the vicious criticism to stop their elixir;
Both of them were malignant to the same extent;
To initiate a battle worth noticing.

-    ***By Kabir Deb***

She is...

Think twice before hurting her

if she was not every time there

you would not be born in this world

nor would have even be able to take a single breath without her

your existence was becoming the biggest challenge for you

if she was not there, you would not be here

Respect her, as she is your mother

If she is elder than you

She makes you calm at hard times

if she is younger than you in the family

she makes you laugh in seconds

relieving you from any stress

Love her as she is your sister.

She is focal point of your life

in many roles that she plays

Of mother, sister, wife or daughter

Adore her, respect her, as she is the ground where you firmly stand.

Why is she not getting her due in the society?

For centuries it happened but now it's a matter of pity

 A big question before whole humanity

After all, where is she...........finally.......?

-   ***By Pallavi Singh***

I Cry

I was sitting in the dark
Just looking for that spark
I saw a demon in that darkness
I got scared from his harshness
He held me tight and told to sit in his lap
I wanted to get up but he shut me up with a slap
I wanted to cry hard
But he told everyone I am a fool, I am a retard
The pain showers down on me from head to toe
I was warned strictly that whatever happens you don't have to
show
I was five when he said, 'You've got such juicy lips
Kiss me hard and I'll tell you about your hips'
Mommy said he was a family friend, a good guy
So talk to him and not be shy
I used to sleep sometimes with that pain
I sat in dark, feeling insane
I finally told Mommy how it was
I cried in sleep and told her who the demon was
She cried and cursed me
But she too told me to be quiet,

whatever happened let it be

she said surprisingly.
My soul was torn apart
I don't know where should I start
Now I am in my twenties and he still comes to our home
I alone know how I control that storm
I wish my Mommy didn't 'shhhh-ed' me that time
I wish had she stayed strong and fought that dirty crime
And here I am sitting in the dark
And still just looking for that spark

By Vinod Gairola

Yes, I am a feminist.

I am a feminist.

Under the sun and amongst the mist,

No matter what world calls me

I'll always want to see women free.

Yes, I am a feminist.

And want to show you all a gist

Of women's strength, courage and power

When all you want to do is shower

Pity and sympathy and build a weak tower.

Yes, I am a feminist.

I want you all to know

That women are not born to bow

In front of your so called norms

And society's wrongly typed forms.

Yes, I am a feminist.

I want all you women to know

That it is time to show.

Not just whine and speak about shine,

But to act for yourself and buy your own wine,

You don't have to just raise the voice

But show that you have made your choice,

Stand up to their shoulder

And show that you can be bolder,

Don't just speak about rights

Stand upright and gear up for your fights.

Yes, I am a feminist.

I want all you women to know

That in the name of feminism,

Don't make a wrong throw

And change the definition of heroism.

Fight for equality

But don't fade away in showing your superiority

For the world is meant to be just

For men and women

And being equal is a must.

Yes, I am a feminist.

I want all you men to know,

That we don't want you to bow,

Carry on with your tasks

But don't try to gift women masks

Appreciate their individuality

And let them make their own way of finding tranquillity;

Yes, I am a feminist.

I want all you men to know

That we don't have any hate to show

We love and support you in different forms

And expect you to do the same in our storms,

We don't want to rule over you

Or turn black all your hues,

But we do hope you to be a little softer

And stop showing that you are physically tougher

You don't have to turn cruel for some vague pleasures

And then act like it is something a woman should treasure.

Yes, I am a feminist.

I want all you humans to know

That rape and molestation can never be a house full show

Be it a woman or a man

You have no right to suppress them in that way

And show that you've had a bright day

You are no one to question their desires

And pretend that they added spark to the fires

Nobody gave you a right over their bodies

And then speak about their bitterness when you are not honeybees.

Yes, I am a feminist.

I want all you parents to know

That it is high time, you stop the puppet show

Treat your child as a child

And not a courageous boy and a girl mild

Don't divide them between pink and blue

And throw their hearts in irrevocable due

Teach your boys to cry and let those emotions out

And let your girls talk aloud,

Don't make periods a taboo

And feminity just a hollow bamboo

Tell them about each gender's struggle

And burst that discrimination bubble

Yes, I am a feminist.

I want all you parents to know

That childhood is like a vow

Teach them to be kind and fair

And not reflect a heart without any care

Teach them to shine and not make each other whine

Show them self-respect and life's positive aspect

Let them know that a man and a woman comes later

A human goes farther

Yes, I am a feminist

And I want you all to be lyricists,

Just like peaceful lyrics

Turn equality to reality, not a part of relics

Show the world the power of women

And let the men be a little more human

Make apologies a part of life

And let not Love turn into strife.

-    *By Tanvi Taparia*

I, woman!

She is a daughter, a sister, a mother, a wife.
It is not easy! A woman's life!

With numerous roles and infinite expectations,
She is the one to unite the generations.

She will love you, respect you, will sacrifice anything for you,
Challenge her self-esteem, and she will destroy you.

A woman is the creator of the world,
Not the one whose life is to be hurled.

The world outside may be a devil for her,
But no one can stop her from moving further.

Lucky are those who are a woman. So proud I'm to be one.
Be humble, be bold, be strong to rule the world and fear none.

-   ***By Sonal Jain***

एक अँधेरी रात

यह कहानी है उस रात की,

वो काली रात जिसमे थी   सिर्फ़ एक आवाज़,

चिला रही थी मै उन सुनसान सड़को पे

लेकिन सुने वाले थे सिर्फ़ दरिंदे

अंदर की आवाज़ कह रही थी की,   'जा भागजा,

पर कुछ हाथो ने रोक लिया था मुझे,

घर पर कर रही थी माँ इतंज़ार

किसने सोचा था बलात्कार होरा है

उसकी लाडली का वहा

चिंतित बाप खड़ा था दरवाज़े पे,

कब आयेगी मेरी परी?   कब आयेगी मेरी परी?

काश कोइ बता देता की सड़क पर हो रहा था

उसका हाल बेहाल,

हाहाकार मचा दिया था पापियो ने,

ना कोई शर्म

ना कोई लिहाज़

आखिर बना दिया उन्होंने मुझे अपना शिकार

एक के बाद,

एक के बाद,

आ गए सब पास

ना जाने क्यों कही खो गई थी मेरी आवाज़

काली थी वो रात

सिर्फ़ और सिर्फ़ अंधेरा था आस-पास

सिर्फ़ और सिर्फ़ अंधेरा था आस-पास...

-    *By Riya Jain*

ना आने की खुशी थी
ना जाने का ग़म था..

ना आने की खुशी थी

ना जाने का ग़म था

ऐसी थी कुछ मेरी कहानी

जिसमे सिर्फ़ और सिर्फ़ दुःख-दर्द था

जिन लोगो ने दिया था जन्म

उन्हीं के हाथों हुआ मरण

जीना था मुझे

जीना था मुझे

कहती थी मै हर दिन

तड़प रही थी उनके प्यार के लिए

लगता था यह ज़िन्दगी मिली है सिर्फ़ मौत जीनेके लिए

दफना दिया जिंदा मुझे ,

आखिर क्या कसूर था मेरा?

ना थी अब कोई पहचान

ना ही कोई आत्मसम्मान.

-   *By Riya Jain*

The Girl Cries

Even they want to spread their wings and fly.
Why don't you just let them try?
This society has become a shackle.
Every day they've got so many eyes to tackle.
All what increases is the shopkeeper's candle production.
Those guys still master their art of seduction.
I wish the mind-set becomes safe,
Instead of filling the minds with chafe.

Even they want to open their wings and fly.
Mentality, would you give it a try?
Why? Why?
Why are women criticised?
Females subjected to foeticide?
XX chromosome, makes you say, "Oh no!".
You say, "Save girls, make them read."
Do you even care? Ever wondered how you treat them?

Knowing all the laws,
Forbidding them all,
Avoiding the thoughts.
You add 'f' to the laws,
And make them flaws.
And after all these, what are your desires?
You want a beautiful intelligent bride.
Who gets you dowry as bribe,
And brings you pride,
Has you inner soul all died??
Wake up! There's still time.
For a stitch which in time could save nine.
Wake up! Keep quiet.
Let them decide what's right.

-   *By Swastik Anand*

Ananya

It is a fine morning or I should say it is the morning she has been waiting for. There was a time when people called her a shameless whore. Maybe she made some mistakes but whatever happened does she really deserve it? She used to cry every night just to wake up next morning to face this world.

"Mistakes." Who doesn't make mistakes? Even God gives equal chance to everyone to commit mistakes. This is how everyone learns but it seemed like her mistakes were unforgiveable.

Ananya was 18 when her life took a beautiful turn. She was selected in one of the top medical colleges of the country. It was the happiest moment of her life. Getting admission in a medical college was her dream and now she was about to live this dream. Moving to a new city and going to college, those thoughts were giving her goose bumps and thrills. She knew her life was going to change and she welcomed these changes with open arms.

Ananya was an inquisitive kind of person, who wanted to explore almost everything. This was the reason she wanted to be a doctor. She wanted to understand how things worked. She was not a total extrovert but she never faced problems in making friends or communicating with others. Like any other teenager in that age, she was attracted to a guy in her college. As time passed, they became good friends and before they knew it they fell in love.

Falling in love was a beautiful experience for her and so was surrendering herself to her beloved. That was the biggest mistake she had made. She was naïve and unprepared to face the consequences. She became pregnant and turned into the subject of discussion for everyone around her. All of a sudden, her life took an ugly turn. Her friends denied talking to her and that guy whom she loved turned his back to her.

Everybody around her was cursing her. Her family members called her a disgrace to all. She always thought and wondered why people were only blaming her. Clearly in this scenario, there was also a guy who was equally involved. This phase was painful for her.

Her family wanted her to return home and even suggested abortion. She was shocked and dejected but she never wanted to abort her unborn child. She decided that she was going to raise the child. This decision of hers infuriated her family and they warned that they would disown her. After seeing all that was happening around her, she never expected her family to support her. But she was determined that her child would see this world and its mother; with or without her family or anyone's support.

She knew she had to complete her education to support herself as well as the child. After this she was unstoppable. She was well aware that nobody would defend her and she had to fight this all alone. She had taken a firm decision and was determined not to let anyone hold the power to hurt her anymore.

She started taking care of herself. After sometime her mother came forward and apologised for her insensitivity. She was the spokesperson at home for Ananya. And finally her father agreed to support his daughter and realised that if he would not be there then he would miss all the happiness which was on its way. Definitely it was a difficult time but they decided to stand by each other's side. Not only her parents but her college also supported her and ensured that Ananya completed her education with all dignity.

Today, after five years of struggle, she is finally getting her degree. It was never easy for her as people asked her about the child's father. It was not easy for her to study alongside the boy who was the father of her child. When he tried to apologise for his deed, she told him that she was not angry with him and that her child does not deserve a spineless man as a father. She was blessed with a beautiful baby daughter.

Today Ananya has made everyone proud - her parents, her daughter and herself. She is truly an inspiring lady, who never gave up her dignity and lived her life like a warrior. No matter what happened she strived through it all bravely. The only man in her life now was her father who was always there. She inspires many girls out there to live their lives with self-respect and dignity.

-   *By Prerna Asthana*

A Letter to Girls

I was told to write about feminism. You know, the usual stuff - equality, respect, women rights, empowerment etc. I remember participating in a debate competition on the same topic and I was against the motion. At that time, I did not realise what women rights or feminism meant. I used to think (under influence of what our elders have taught us) that women at one point of time, take advantage of their freedom. Now, do not get me wrong. I am a woman myself, a mother of two beautiful children. I totally support woman empowerment. I just had not understood the concept of the said topic at that time.

Today, when I am no longer in college and have entered a practical world, I come across certain societal problems which are basically inherent from the stupid mentality. Asking a woman to stay in her limits, telling her to wear decent clothes that, you know, hide her provocative parts (as if they did not know that!!), not allowing her to go out after 10 unless she was with her husband, her brother or her father.

I am still not well versed with the concept of feminism but now, I do feel that women deserve an equal place in comparison to men. From giving birth to a human being, to setting her foot on Mars, I believe, and I know that women have encountered all possible fears, broken the bounds and dodged many remarks that could make her belief in herself shake.

Surprisingly most of the times, it's the other women around her that waver her faith in herself. Be it either the mother or mother-in-law. The mother of a son opines that she will bring a daughter-in-law for her home who will do all the chores of the house, entertain guests, massage her feet at night before sleeping, listen to her husband and never question anything.

I want to ask those women, if their own parents taught them the same. Was massaging their mother-in-law's feet their dream?

Did they dream of spending all their lives listening to their husbands' bullshit, in-law's rebukes, and children's curses?

I do not say that marriage is bad. But the place of a woman in a marriage is barely recognisable, even in today's world. When a girl gets married, she is taught to remain silent when elders are talking, while her husband who is barely two years elder to her is allowed to put his opinions before others.

Don't you think it's really unacceptable nonsense? When cowardice and remaining silent is being taught at home, what will a girl do when the time comes to stand up for herself? Gladly, there are millions of women who know who they are, what their ambitions are, what they want to achieve in their lives and are really, really bad mouthed. Because, they know people around them are not as wise as they appear to be. They know that people will take your politeness for granted and suppress you when the time comes.

This is to all the girls who are still waiting for their Prince Charming to take over their lives' peace.

Please, please, please! Do not ruin your life over some imaginary man! Take charge of it and lead it onto the path where you can create wonders. Have that passion in you which keeps burning until you become something. Do not let the struggles douse the fire of your passion to make something of yourself. You are a woman, and you are more than worth it!

That was about the motivational part. Now, coming to reality. Life is not going to be easy. They are going test your patience, your forbearance. Make sure they are worth your time. Be strong and wise enough to learn life lessons from those people who have let you down or did not let you get up. Never let anyone's opinions about you falter your way. Have faith in yourself because you know you can overcome any hurdle standing in your way. You came out of your mother's womb with so much difficulty that any person going through the same pain could die. But when you were put in her arms, she had smiled. Learn from this very occurrence, that a woman will undergo any extreme pain and still smile. That is something only a woman can do.

I am not a feminist. I am an 'equalist'. I believe that women have their own dreams that can bloom into wondrous feats. They do not need to wait for the opportunities or a charity that you will give them the chance to grow. They will go out on their ways to achieve what they have set in their minds and you will keep looking at their success and feel jealous.

All the men out there, if you think, women are supposed to be in the kitchen, remember, that is where they keep knives. Provoke them and you will know what real pain is. People must not say that it is just the man who earns. I have met and been in company of several women who have employed people.

I know women who know the value of dreams and never once will they let you feel that yours is any less. They will inspire you to go beyond your comfort zone and break out all the limits only to make you realise your vision. I respect those ladies out there who are both emotionally and mentally strong!

I know this is not a debate competition, nor a platform for a motivational speech, but I could not resist venting my heart out on the topic that is still misunderstood in many parts of our own country. To conclude my write-up, I'd say to the young women out there - Live young and work hard. Embrace the hardships and show the world, YOU are invincible.

-    *By Preiksha Jain*

Dear Zindegi, A wish.

When I walked into the living room, I witnessed a usual scene from a usual Indian household. The television running in the living room without an audience, welcomed me. I searched for the book, which I had left there the previous night. It was on the table. I picked the remote and switched off the television set.

"Who switched off the TV?" a shout boomed in the house from the bedroom. It must be them; some had probably stayed back after the IPL match. They, who are invited anytime - my sisters' friends.

I turned the television on and sat there on the sofa holding the book, trying to be an audience. One by one they came into the living room. My sisters' friends greeted me; I returned the wishes with a smile. My sister looked at the book I was holding and dart a 'You-always-hold-a-book' look. Yes, most of the time I do, I smiled at her too.

I tuned the TV to NatGeo People channel, where a series was being telecast called 'Indian Hotels'. Every one of us got glued to the screen, because they were featuring a snippet on THE TAJ Hotels, Mumbai. Yes, the famous one near the Gateway of India. I don't know why, but I am quite fascinated by the grandeurs of its architecture and have a secret wish to take my family inside that gigantic structure and have a cup of tea. I made a mental note.

"She is beautiful," said my sister. "And young too!" I shot back. They giggled when I said that. I was surprised because I hadn't giggled when they commented. We were talking about the host of that show, Nazeera, the Deputy Manager of the Hotels. One of my sister's friends tried to join our tête-à-tête by spitting the following, "Yeah, young and beautiful, that's why she is on the top position. I don't see any other skill that qualifies her for that position." We all looked at her puzzled.

Her thoughts triggered another incident that had happened at our office cafeteria. All of us in the team, my colleagues and I, were having this tasteless beverage vended by the coffee machine. We opt for that life killing drinks because the gossips we have are delicious. We talked about almost everything and everybody. Then this girl named Anamika walked past our table. Suddenly, a colleague of mine sitting at the table named Aparna added to our gossip list - may be topping the chart for the day. She disclosed that Anamika had compromised on 'something' to get the Assistant Manager's position, though she had less experience. That comment had got some exclamations and ooohs and aaahs from all. But I had remained silent in my thoughts. Like I had done today.

I was grounded back to our living room by a slap on my thigh. "Day dreamer, we are going to make noodles, you want some?" It was my sister. They always ask this, though they very well know that I'm not an instant noodle person. I would rather prefer water. I know that when Mom is out of town and it happens to be a Sunday then the menu on breakfast is by default 'Noodles.' I don't have complaints, because I know that it's the only day they get to relax. I am worried about the ill effects the noodles can have on us, another Chinese invasion which is going to cost us dearly.

I said, "No, I will make some milkshake. May be later! Now, let me finish this book, you guys carry on."

The television was still running. I kept the remote on the table and walked to my room. My sisters and their friends were in the kitchen, muscling their way to make the 2 minutes wonder breakfast.

When I got into my room, some bizarre thoughts kept hitting me. Why is it, that if a woman achieves something astonishing in her career, she has to be judged? Why don't we talk about men in the same way? What if she had climbed the ladder of success because she was the best in the business? What if she really is talented? It's not easy to fake the skills required to reach and be at that position. It is not the first time I was experiencing such reeking comments or thoughts being hurled in my presence but I was always left questioning - why are we so judgmental?

I opened the book; it was a book having the world's greatest speeches. Removing the bookmark, I started reading.

'THE ONLY QUESTION LEFT TO BE SETTLED NOW IS: ARE WOMEN PERSONS? AND I HARDLY BELIEVE ANY OF OUR OPPONENTS WILL HAVE THE HARDIHOOD TO SAY THEY ARE NOT. BEING PERSONS, THEN, WOMEN ARE CITIZENS; AND NO STATE HAS A RIGHT TO MAKE ANY LAW OR TO ENFORCE ANY OLD LAW, THAT SHALL ABRIDGE THEIR PRIVILEGES OR IMMUNITIES.'

I believe that women are fighting among themselves. Yes, they are their own opponents. A woman is much better than a man yet if she feels second class, she is lowering her standards; she is bringing disgrace to herself.

I wish, Susan B Anthony the orator of the above speech comes to life from year 1873 to our time and sees what has changed. From second class citizens, the change has put them in a position to wage a battle within themselves. I wish cataloguing the gender with profession gets lost in the mist of atonements.

Next time when we see a successful person, let us appreciate their efforts, the hard work they put in to conquer their hurdles, the sweat that has gone in reaching and maintaining that position and also thank them, for showing us that it can be achieved by anyone of us by channelling our energy in the right direction.

"Hey, they are showing your favourite movie of Alia!!" I could sense my sister's excitement in breaking the news to me.

Getting up from the bed, I kept the book on my wooden table. Leashing the thoughts in my mind I walked into the living room, the title cards were already flashing.

PS: In the 1800s women in the United States had few legal rights and did not have the right to vote. The excerpts I used in BOLD are from the inspiring speech by SUSAN B ANTHONY given after her arrest for casting an illegal vote in the presidential election of 1872.

- *By Josh, Independent filmmaker*